Mothers, Myths and Memories

Personal Tales of love, loss and the lives we carry

AF663969

PAYAL SHANDIL GUPTA

BlueRose ONE.com
Stories Matter
NewDelhi • London

BLUEROSE PUBLISHERS
India | U.K.

BlueRose ONE.com
Stories Matter
New Delhi • London

For permissions requests or inquiries regarding this publication, please contact:

BLUEROSE PUBLISHERS
www.BlueRoseONE.com
info@bluerosepublishers.com
+91 8882 898 898
+4407342408967

ISBN: 978-93-7310-018-0

Cover design: Yash Singhal
Typesetting: Namrata Saini

First Edition: September 2025

Contents

Why Do I Write?

A simple thought or perhaps just a single word may drift into your mind as you sit back, enjoying a cuppa on a warm sunny afternoon. Or, a stranger might capture your attention unexpectedly. This sensation is fleeting, almost like experiencing the comforting warmth of a hug from someone you haven't seen in years. You cling to this moment, wishing to extend its duration as though you're trying to hold onto the delightful flavour of hot chocolate lingering in your mouth long after the cup has been set aside and cleaned.

The thoughts begin to flow like words being strung together into a beautiful pearl necklace–elegant yet slightly restrictive. You find yourself toying with these ideas, allowing your fingertips to glide over the smooth contours of the pearls, all the while secretly relishing the cool sensation they bring. Some thoughts appeal to you, while others, you let slip away. But through it all that initial word or concept continues to echo in the background. Eventually, you pick up a pen and some paper, ready to unleash the quiet torrent of creativity that has been building up within you and the story begins.

The Pilgrimage

The screams drowned all the other sounds, the glass shattering into a million pieces on contact with unrelenting metal, metal being dragged over metal, bones being crushed and bodies falling on the concrete. She clung to her husband's arm, but the crushing weight of bodies tore them apart. Panicked, she searched for him, but the chaos swallowed him whole. Her shouts had no effect on anyone. She moved in the direction the crowd pushed her, grasping for air praying she would soon reach an open space. Something tugged at her dupatta, constricting her. She pulled to release it. Her efforts were in vain. The weight of bodies continued to push her, tightening the dupatta around her neck like a deadly noose. Suddenly, without warning, the dupatta came loose and she fell forward. Her foot landed on something soft, and she looked down. Lifeless eyes of a middle-aged man stared back at her with a half-eaten apple in his hand. Shocked, she lifted her foot and stepped on the side. It was a mistake. She stumbled and the crowd shoved her to the ground. She tried to get up and move aside, but there was no escape. Feet pounded over her, pinning her down. Her cries vanished beneath the deafening chaos. "Please take care of Keshu," she gasped as another foot pressed her face into the concrete.

Keshu sat still, confused, afraid to move. His grandmother clutched his hand. She was crying endlessly, occasionally wrapping her arms around him. Her sobs grew lounder each time she hugged him. All his relatives were there, most of them crying too. Many patted his head, gave him blessings and called him a poor boy. He was hungry, but something told him not to ask his grandmother for food. He wished his mother could come soon. She always made the best yummiest breakfasts for him. He was never hungry when she was around. " Come say goodbye to your parents" someone said, leading him into the courtyard, gently holding his hand. " Ma and Pa?" Keshu asked brightening up. Ma had said she would get lots of blessings for him. He did not know what blessings were, something to eat or something to play with- but was sure it was something he would love. Keshu did not understand when they stopped in front of something wrapped in white sheets. That could not be 'blessings'. His grandmother collapsed on the bundle calling him. "Say goodbye to your mother" she cried, holding his hand. He resisted. "No! This is not Ma, she told me she will be back on Tuesday, it is not Tuesday today. She went to the big Mela to get special blessings for me" Keshu jerked his grandmother's hand away and ran back in the house. The big white bundle with flowers on it was not his mother. She always wore bright clothes with dupatta, and smelled of cardamom - his favourite smell in the world. She loved cooking, playing with him and going to the market with his grandmother. She was not the still bundle lying in the courtyard. It was not his mother. He would sit in his room, hungry and alone till she came home.

Karma

"Focus on the your labour, not on the fruits of that labour" You told Arjuna before You guided him to victory. He was a scared, unsure man, and you lead him on the path to righteousness, victory and glory.

But what of me? I see no path in front of me. I stand here directionless, purposeless and uncertain of my future. Leading warriors to battles, leading revolutions or even holding down a humble job to provide for my family is not my fate. I am not even the tiny droplet that falls from the sky to quench the thirst of the parched earth. I am just a person who follows the sun, morning to night and night to morning. I end my day exactly where I began it. Did you forget me O'Krishna? Does the page for my karma lie blank in your book? Was I sent to this life only to enjoy the fruits of other's karma? Always the receiver, never the giver? Is this my fate – to gradually fade into nothingness?

He smiled, he let me finish my lamentation without interruption. He waited as tears rolled down my face. He calmly watched as I climbed out of the pit of misery I had dug for myself. Finally he said, "A hunter with a quiver filled with arrows and a farmer with a plow and fertile land shall remain hungry till they use their tools. The hunter needs to search and hunt his prey and the farmer needs to till his land. Look around you, the talents , the skills, the resources you have, they ask you the same question you ask me. What is their purpose? Their path? Their destiny? Like you, they receive no reply. You are not purposeless. You have a path ahead, a direction, a destiny. You can't see it because you haven't paved it yet. You can be something, anything or nothing – this is your battleground. I sit here patiently holding the reigns of your chariot. I can drive in any direction you desire, but I can't fight this battle for you.

The Tree

The shirt landed half on the bed and half on the floor, right next to the other two shirts he had just discarded. He knew his wife would grumble about the shirts and wet towel on the bed, but he couldn't care less. He looked in the mirror; did his hair depict the frustration and helplessness he felt? Did his eyes give away the fact that he had wept well into the night, long after his wife and kids went to bed? His young daughter sometimes refused a good night hug and kiss. "Pa, your breath stinks," she would say, crinkling up her cute tiny nose. He rinsed his mouth again not wanting anyone to speculate if he had an extra drink or two to cope with the devastating news. The news that he would be jobless by the end of the month.

Seventeen years of backbreaking work had earned him a small severance and seventeen days of notice. Outside, the world carried on, like nothing had changed. Perhaps the only one who could empathize with him was the tree outside his window. A few short weeks earlier its branches groaned under the weight of its fruits. It was full of life; birds, squirrels, happy kids and a million insects sought food, shelter and comfort in its branches. And now, the tree was barren, no fruit hung from its branches, its leaves fell with the lightest of the breeze, and it had neither food nor shelter to offer.

In many ways, just a few hours ago, he was like the tree he thought –full of life, brimming with ideas and ambition. He was the manager, the team leader whom everyone admired and sought to emulate. Now, like the tree, he stood by, watching the last leaves fall.

A brief email from his boss had turned his professional life topsy turvy and made it turbulent. Although there had been rumors, he had dismissed them, confident in his work and strong work ethic. He was too busy dedicating himself to the company he had invested so much in, pouring his heart and soul into every project. "Winter will be here soon," he told the tree, hoping for a reply.

The tree stood tall, not shaken by the gusts of wind that took away more leaves. The tree had been there for long before he was born. It stood there proud and tall. He seen it over the years in every season and weather many storms. His grandfather had built the house in the trees shadow. 'The tree did not fear the future nor lament about the past'. The man smiled. Yes, like the tree the spring was behind him. Undoubtedly, the times had been good, but there was nothing to gain by sheading tears over what had happened. It would be painful to see the next stage unfold at work, but he was strong. He turned away from the tree, his contemplation and self-doubt disappearing, and picked the discarded shirts and the wet towel. He even made the bed, just the way his wife liked it. Spring was over, but the winter did not scare him. Like the tree his branches were strong and high, and his roots were deep. He could weather the storm that was brewing and brave the winter that lay ahead. Like the tree, he knew that spring and a bright summer waited for him around the corner.

The Prison

Is it a prison if you hold the keys in your hand?

She stood there on the threshold ready to take flight, frozen in time. She had big dreams and aspirations, but her fears robbed the wind from under her wings. So she stood there, just ready to take flight yet, her feet remained cemented to the floor. 'What happens if I fail? Worse, if my dreams are not worth achieving? What of the sacrifices required?' The doubts and the questions were ceaseless.

One could say it was the comfort that kept her locked within. She had roof over her head and food on her table. Food, a place to sleep, clothing and a few luxuries, the basic comforts of life were guaranteed. Was that enough though? The everyday life grated off her essence, day by day, layer by layer. She felt that one day there would be nothing of her left, just an empty shell, existing.

She took a deep breath and opened the door. The fresh, cool air brought in confidence and hope. She flapped her wings and took flight. As she soared into the vastness above, the weight of her uncertainties began to dissolve, replaced by the exhilarating realization that true freedom lay not in the absence of fear but in the courage to confront it head-on. With each beat of her new found wings she got closer to what she could be and further away from an abusive husband.

The Unknown Neighbour

The light in the window of the building across caught her eye. She looked at the wall clock, her trusted and silent keeper of time. “Strange, they don't wake up so soon,” she thought to herself. The fact that it was winter break and their kid wouldn’t be going to school, made it odd. "Maybe they are off for a vacation." However, the lack of any visible travel preparations made her doubt this explanation.

She could see the silhouette of someone moving about as she began her day. The unhurried, determined movements of the unknown man were mesmerizing. As the unknown man continued with his tasks, moving from one room to another; was it the husband? She could not tell. Something was off. She knew for a fact that the husband was a smoker and started his day with a quick smoke on the balcony even on the chilliest and the windiest days. This person was not the husband. The thought that a stranger might be in her neighbours’ apartment made her stomach tighten with dread.

In between her coffee, chopping, grinding and cooking, her mind kept flitting back to the window. Try as she may, she could not shake away that feeling. There was nothing that suggested any cause of worry. The man and his deliberate movements around the house suggested no hurry or alarm. "Maybe he is a friend, or a brother." That would explain so many things, including the fact that he was up and about before the others, yet the inexplicable sense of unease within her refused to dissipate. It was eight, time for tea with her husband. She made the tea and took it to the living room away from the window facing her neighbours. She needed to pull herself away from obsessing over the strange early light in a stranger's home.

She did not know the family. They lived in the building across, but she had seen them often eating or playing and once spring-cleaning their home during summer. She knew they were a family of three, a husband, wife and young daughter. The stroller was often parked near the large glass door to the balcony. She had often seen the mother and daughter play on the balcony in the sweltering summer. Those moments always made her feel a little nostalgic. The times when she played with her kids. The clutter, the messy kitchen and the heaps of toys in the house filled with the laughter of kids were a blessing that she missed.

The onset of winter drove everyone inside. Weirdly, she missed the family. The comfort of strangers sharing a daily routine was warm and reassuring. Yet, today the feeling was different. 'Something was wrong' her heart kept saying. But she had no means to find out or to offer help. She may feel that she knew the family, but she did not exist in their world.

The Second Slice

The birthday cake had been cut, the gifts unwrapped, and the guests had all gone home. She sat on the couch beside her uncle, working her way through a second slice of cake. She was nearly full, so this piece disappeared slowly.

"What do you want to be when you grow up?" her uncle asked.

Her mother always said it was rude to talk with food in your mouth, so she quickly swallowed. "I'll be a big manager like Papa or Kavita Aunty. I'll go to office every morning in my big car and work on a nice purple laptop."

She paused to take another bite. "I won't work on Saturdays, Sundays, or Diwali. And my office will give me a big house to live in."

She loved talking–and talking about herself was her favourite thing.

"I could also be a teacher like Diya Miss," she added between bites. She had a captive audience and wasn't about to let small things–like cake in her mouth–interrupt her flow.

"I'll teach kids in school. They'll all love me, and their parents will like me too. I'll get angry when they don't do their homework, but I won't punish them. I'll give them chocolates when they get 10 out of 10 on a test. But I don't–"

She froze mid-sentence, fork halfway to her mouth.

Her uncle raised an eyebrow. She shrugged, popped the bite into her mouth, and continued.

"No, I don't think I'll be a teacher. It's nice that kids will love me and listen to me. But I won't have a nice car like Papa, or a big house like Kavita Aunty."

She may only be ten, but she already understood the difference between a profession and a vocation.

Homecoming

The thing about returning home is that everyone looks at you with unmistakable admiration. After all, you are amongst the few who made it and big moved abroad.

Just that in my case, it is misplaced admiration. I moved not because I earned an admission in a prestigious university, or a job, or a promotion; I simply moved with my much talented and successful husband.

Life across the oceans is certainly better in so many ways- lesser crime, smoother roads, better stocked shelves in the shops and supermarkets, education and healthcare. The new landscape has much to offer, each weather change is an adventure, and each sunset is new. How can I forget the clean air and the low AQI?

And back home?

I befriended a toddler unabashedly shared her plan for the day with me, a total stranger, while her mother smiled, enjoying our banter. I lost the security tags to my shopping bags in the shopping mall and a smile was enough for the security guard to hand me the bags. I joked with the sales assistants and each one of them got my jokes. Something that is yet to happen in my adopted country. The guy at the food stall needed barely any verbal instructions to understand how I wanted my plate. In case you are wondering, the pav bhaji was perfect just the way I liked it -slightly spicy, a little sweet, served with a little garnish of onion slices and a wedge of lemon on the side.

The roads were congested, but I knew where exactly I could hail a cab. I was not an outsider looking in, but a part of the crowd. I jumped into conversations with unacquainted people to offer my two cents. Smiles were returned with bigger smiles.

So, the next time you meet someone who person has who made it and is living life king size, throw in a little kindness with your admiration for they are missing what you have.

Band of Women

Two stones, one painted gold, a walnut, an incomplete fox, a toy car, a chew toy, two beads, a white pipping nozzle, a diary, a mirror and a bee on a clip. Each representing the women sitting around in the circle. Hope, desires, aspirations, and dreams all boiled down to one single object.

If you look at the objects, it is difficult to imagine that they could create something together, but they did, just like the women they represented.

What brought the women together? Was it the age or culture? No. The women came from different cultures - Hungary, Austria, Russia and India; spoke different languages - Hungarian, French, Russian, English, Hindi; and were in different stages in life - a new mother, a wife struggling to keep her marriage together and another starting her business. The thread that connected them was motherhood.

They were all mothers stepping out of the shadow of parenthood to rediscover themselves. All of them loved their kids and agreed that being a mother was the greatest blessing of all. It was time to accept that and take a step beyond the threshold of motherhood. An exciting point to be on, yet scary. So they held hands and took the step forward. It was not easy - inch by inch, pushing and pulling, they moved forward. There were tears, and laughter; pain and pleasure, up and downs, and all through that they never let go and held on to their newfound belief in themselves.

I could write the end, but their journey has just started.

Beyond a Mother's Reach

Sputnik ran away last week. My baby, the apple of my eye—my puppy—ran away!

The doorbell rang. The door opened. And he was out like a bullet.

Usually, this wouldn't be a big concern. For my darling—*always a puppy, never a dog*—it's just a game. He runs, and someone runs after him. If you're not fast enough, he even waits for you, tilting his cute little head in mock concern.

Unfortunately, I lost precious seconds dealing with the stranger at the door. It was the lady from upstairs, and I was forced to play the part of the nice, polite neighbour while she explained the reason for her visit.

Minutes later, I was in the neighbour's garden. I walked up and down the flower beds, climbed the stairs, looked around—expecting to see him, because he loved hanging out with the little ones there. But as time passed, and Sputnik didn't appear, a sinking feeling set in.

If we lost Sputnik, the blame would squarely fall on me. I had never taught him to respond to "*Come back!*" I always told myself I'd do it tomorrow. I regretted never taking him to the big dog park, just a little farther from home. There, he could have learned a thing or two from the older, better-behaved dogs. But I never had the time.

My worry grew, my throat raw from calling out, my voice growing louder and more desperate with every passing minute. He was just a young puppy—out in the dark, without a leash, in unfamiliar territory. I pictured him on a grand little adventure, blissfully unaware that he was lost. He didn't know that the world beyond our fence wasn't always kind... or safe.

With help from two kind neighbours, a watchful guard, and a wait that felt like forever—forty long minutes—Sputnik was back in his cozy bed, happily munching on a snack, blissfully unaware of the chaos he had caused.

That got me thinking.

The doorbells will keep ringing. My kids will keep stepping out. To me, they will always be too young, too innocent, too naïve. But the world will never see them through my eyes. They will walk their own paths, seek their own adventures—and I won't always be there. It's my job to prepare them. The feeling of not doing enough will always weigh on my heart. But starting today, I'm going to set things right. We'll start small—little things like doing their laundry and packing their lunch. I can't childproof the world. But the next time they dash out the door, they'll know how to look after themselves.

Or, when things get a little too much... they'll call Supermom.

When I Grow Up...

"How was school?" Shaya grabbed the school bag before it hit the floor.

"Okay, I studied and ate lunch. Tara did not come to school." Madhu did not pause as she skipped to the dining table. " I wrote an essay on 'what I want to be when I grow up."

"O' that is interesting. So, what do you want to be? A ballerina? No. An astronaut? No?" Shaya put a sandwich in front of Madhu. Technically, it was just bread and butter, but the she had cut the crust also off and also cut the slices into triangles because Madhu loved it that way. "Let me think – I know you want to be a doggie doctor!"

"You are funny mum. I want to be a Mum when I grow up." Madhu grabbed the sandwich and took an enthusiastic bite into the buttery sandwhich her eyes sparkling with a mix of innocence and determination.

"A mum? Why? And don't talk with food in your mouth."

"Sorry mum". She swallowed the bite and placed the rest of the sandwich back on the plate. This was serious talk. "Because, mums are superheroes. You work in an office, make the yummiest food, like this boat sandwich and help me with my homework. You even scared naughty Tom when he was bullying me."

"That is a long list, my dear. But I can't do everything."

"I know. You can't sing. You are the most horrid singer ever. But that is okay; Supergirl can't sing either."

It was difficult not to smile at her daughter's logic. "Or Spiderman?"

"Or Spiderman." Madhu agreed. " But I don't like him anymore. Tara said he has a girlfriend. Ewww ! Mum, I like you-you are the best."

"I like you too, my kiddo. You are the bestest."

"Shivani Miss said bestest is not a word" Madhu paused. "Can I ask you a question, mum?"

"You may ask a question, my love." Shaya kept Madhu's school bag on the table and walked towards the kitchen with the lunch box and water bottle.

"You are a good people and the best mommy. You don't even have a girlfriend like Spiderman. Why did daddy leave you?"

Lighter

Yesterday was a revelation. I was in a training and the trainer introduced a training activity which involved walking on a rope while other trainees supported me. When the trainer said one could opt out of the activity, I was one of the first ones to raise my hands.

For those who don't know me, I am a horizontally challenged person and though people falling on me would appreciate my fluffy body for safety, me falling on them would be an unwelcome and rather unpleasant experience.

So rather than giving the other team members the opportunity to say no to support me, I opted out. Midway the activity a participant asked me if I would be next. The excitement in her eyes was contiguous and without much thought I said yes. And it was more than any words can express. I did the activity not once but twice!

In the end the trainer asked if others if supporting me was any different than supporting others. The answer was a loud no.

This was it, I realised it was not my weight holding me back, it was me. I cared too much about what the others saw and thought and forgot the most important person, me. All those missed dances, the dresses I did not try, the games I watched from the sidelines. what a waste I summarise. And without weighing a gram less, I am feel as light as the clouds in the sky.

Winter, I Hate Thee

"I don't appreciate the heat of summers, nor the showers that the rainy season brings—and I hate winters," I declare to anyone with ears and two minutes to spare.

Then, one beautiful year, I experienced winter in all its splendour.

The entire landscape transformed into a brilliant white, reminiscent of the most exquisite Christmas card—a scene only Van Gogh could have captured. The trees stood tall and proud in their bare beauty, while the sky was a vivid blue, dotted with fluffy white clouds. The whole world seemed to hold its breath, as if afraid to disturb the flawless calm. I admired it all from the warmth of my cozy home and wondered: *Did this moment challenge my long-held belief that I disliked the cold, the dampness, and the dreariness that winter always represented for me?*

Armed with a thick jacket and a warm scarf, I decided to find out.

The roads were wet and slippery from the recent snow. The frost and melt had created delicate patterns on the sidewalk—beautiful enough to be worth a fall or two. The trees looked like diamond chandeliers, their icicles catching the light as they hung precariously from bare branches. The myriad footprints on the fresh snow looked like a map to hidden treasure. Even the icy wind was a gift—it shook off my lethargy and filled me with a new kind of energy, the kind that makes you feel alive. Snow had blanketed everything ugly and unwanted, turning the world into a wonderland I didn't want to leave.

I **love** winters.

There are so many things in life we dismiss too quickly. We decide we dislike something without ever scratching beneath the surface.

Today, go out and scratch the surface of your winter. Who knows what treasures await?

Procrastinators' Lounge

"I am a procrastinator."

I feel no pride or shame when I say this. That's just the way I am. I move to tomorrow what could easily be done today. Why?

There are numerous theories about this. My dad attributes it to laziness. Naturally, I don't share that view. A motivational speaker I once encountered suggested it was self-sabotage (which was her term of the week !) I used to think it was a hereditary trait but my parents are the kind who always complete tomorrow's tasks today, and my grandparents didn't have the luxury of being punctual or procrastinating. However, my favourite uncle is like me. We are two souls cut from the same fabric. The remaining theories explaining procrastination include fear of failure and lack of appreciation for time. They may be true, but not always.

Over the years I realized that none of these theories are a hundred percent wrong, except the speaker- she was definitely 110% wrong. Procrastination and procrastinators are much more than these descriptions. In fact, they are actually workaholics.

Yep, they are workaholics, *they just don't have enough work!* As a solution, they wait till they have 26 hours of work and only 20 hours to complete it. O' the thrill of working non-stop, to missed calls and quick lunches on the go. The sleepless nights, the clatter of fingers flying off the keyboard and the aching neck. It is a high you never want to come down from.

So how come I am sitting and writing these thoughts? Well, my boss just moved up a deadline and gave me another project to squeeze into the same deadline. The almonds I soaked for a cake are ready, and I plan to bake a shepherd's pie for dinner today. What better day than today to justify how a procrastinator's mind works? But first - the ceiling fans need cleaning!!

Half Unicorn, Whole Me

The horn and the hair are done. I must say, purple suits you far more than that dowdy brown.

Now hold out your paws, dear–they'll make the most magnificent hooves.

"Hmmm..."

"It won't hurt a bit. Don't be afraid. Just hold them out."

"I was just wondering... maybe you could leave the ears? And my paws too? Please?"

"WHAT?!" Fairy Godmothers don't raise their voices–but right now, she didn't care.

"A unicorn with paws and a bear face? That's simply not possible." She paused to take a calming breath. "You've dreamed of being a unicorn your whole life. Now's your chance!"

"But I am a bear. And if you help me, I can be a unicorn too."

"It's either one or the other–it can never be both."

"Why does the world always push me into a pigeonhole? Why do I have to give up parts of myself? I like my paws. My small, round ears." He touched his ears for reassurance. "This big, huggable tummy. They make me me. Yes, I want to be a unicorn—but I don't want to lose everything else I love just to get there."

The Fairy Godmother blinked. No one had ever talked back before. She was the Fairy Godmother. The one who made dreams come true. She had turned maids into princesses, frogs into princes—no doubts, no questions. "This is the way of the world, my dear," she finally said, gently. "Bears are bears, and unicorns are unicorns."

"But... aren't we all a little bit of both? Isn't Rosie Indian and a bit American? She loves both paranthas and pancakes for breakfast. When her father makes breakfast for her mother, isn't he both a CEO and a loving husband? Didn't his company just win an award, and his pancakes the 'Super Best'? What about the little boy who plays with dolls and dreams of dragons? And you—aren't you both a Fairy Godmother and a queen?"

The Good Asian Mother

My daughter's friend just got back from her Korean and Math classes at the weekend school. While at home, my dearest daughter just about rolled out of bed and finished breakfast. Unlike many of her classmates, she does not attend any classes after school. Neither does she have a list of a hundred books to read during summer vacation. None of these other kids are geniuses or prodigies and the effort other mothers put in with the kids is clearly visible in the stack of certificates and trophies the possessed. My daughter, she is cut from a different cloth. Mine went to the school admission interview with her personality and a cute empty bag. "Indian kids usually come with a stack full of certificates for extra-curricular activities," the school counsellor mentioned, trying very unsuccessfully to hide her surprise.

My efforts for my daughter and her future seem rather insignificant compared to those of the other mums from India or, the rest of Asia. Our household doesn't have a constant flurry of activities, running from school to activities and to more activities. Meal times and bedtimes are flexible. French fries with ketchup could be lunch or breakfast. Once every couple of months, we skip school to go out for a movie and lunch—not for a birthday or a special occasion—just on a random day. Those are the days when homework, tests, and the few after-school activities we have don't exist.

I tell my daughter to be happy and satisfied with her circumstances. I tell her she needs to earn money if she wants a life of luxury, or prepare for a tough life if she finds more valuable pursuits. Rich or poor, I teach her to be healthy and safe. She is taught to be polite, and she even helps around in the house. She reads when she feels like it and picks up a painting brush once in six months. I can see a lot of potential boiling under the surface, she could be a painter or would absolutely rock the world with her pen. It is my job to hand her the right tools and it is her's to harness her potential.

Unlike other moms, I'm not overly worried about the grades she gets as long as she's comfortable sharing them with others. I tell her that if she feels embarrassed about her performance, she should put in more effort. The timing and method are things she figures out on her own. She ends up getting everything she wants and a little extra. We talk, we share, we offer a shoulder to cry on to each other.

However, everything said and done, as an Asian mom, I feel I should do a bit more. Maybe a short trip to the kitchen? Mums are known to cook healthy meals for their kids. Meals that feed the soul and the body. Maybe we can have fries with cheese instead of roti and sabzi and call it a soul night !

The Race that Mattered

The little girl was in tears as she ran into her father's arms. She had tried her best—she'd practiced, and she ran as fast as her tiny legs could carry her. She didn't stop, even when her lungs felt like they were about to burst.

But it was all in vain. She hadn't won the race—again. "Winning is not important, dear," her father consoled her. "What matters is that you ran." She wanted very much to believe him.

I wish I could tell you those early defeats lit a fire in her—and with hard work and her father's support, she went on to become an athlete and brought home an Olympic gold.

But that's not what happened. Not even close.

Something better did.

Our little girl grew up. She was ordinary, average, forgettable even. Good at a few things, bad at a few others. She seemed destined to live and die without a trace—like millions of women around her. Then, somewhere along the way, something changed.

She stopped trying to squeeze into the world's expectations and began carving her own path—in school, at work, and in life. She did things she wanted to and in the way she believed was right. Not everyone agreed. They called her foolish. Stubborn. They warned her that her path would lead to disappointment and failure.

But she kept going anyway. Her happiness mattered more than the noise of other people's opinions–she kept reminding herself.

And then, one morning, she walked into work and found her desk buried under flowers. Dozens of them. Her students, their parents, and her colleagues had come together to show their appreciation. She wasn't just a teacher. She was *the* teacher.

The one who went the extra mile.

The one who always listened.

The one with a warm smile and a helping hand. The one other teachers turned to for advice.

She may have lost countless races–as a child, and even as an adult–But she won the one that truly mattered.

Eyes that Truly See

"What do you see?"

"Hmm.
I see a young woman robbed of a happy, normal life. Dreams and hopes for the future, snatched away—replaced with a burden too big and too heavy for her delicate shoulders. So much potential, buried under the harsh realities of life."

"Do you want to know what I see in this picture? I see a beautiful young woman, smiling and soaking in the sun. She may appear delicate, even fragile—but look closely. Notice the way she sits: straight-backed, eyes steady, looking ahead without fear. She has the will, the strength, and the wits to overcome whatever life—or maybe even you—choose to throw her way. She carries dreams, hopes, and desires. And one day, she will turn them into reality."

"You worry that you may never learn to love her. What's funny is—you don't even see her.

All you see is yourself: the reluctant saviour, rescuing her and the nation for a doomed fate. But she—in her pink dress, with her messy hair and muddy flats—she is the saviour. For you. And for the country you and I claim to love so deeply."

The Bra Strap

Our first meeting was not pleasant. I hated wearing it. It was complicated, uncomfortable, and, moreover, something to be ashamed of.

I spent my teens hiding the fact that I needed one—worse, that I wore one. Long opaque slips, safety pins, and higher necklines—anything to hide the culprit. And the world around me wholeheartedly agreed. I once got an earful from my landlady because a neighbour saw them hanging out to dry. I was nineteen when the scary incident happened. The neighbour and my landlady were traumatized by my carelessness—and by the sight of my hated companion hanging on a clothesline for the world to see.

I grew up, and fortunately, so did my relationship with the strap. I could still spot one from a mile away, but now it was different. A swanky strap peeking out from a smart top—on purpose. A strap at the end of a winning basketball game. An ill-fitting strap. And the strap with pearls that I covet.

A single strap—well, a pair, if we're being sticklers for tiny details—began a revolution in my mind and changed my life.

Now I'm a mum, and today is the day my daughter and I go shopping. She's a big girl now and needs one. So what do I tell my daughter?

"Say hello to your new friend—the bra. Your body needs extra support, and this one takes care of you, just like the special shoes Papa wears to the gym!"

Listen to Your Mother

Both of us were women and the children of the late seventies but this is where all the similarities ended. She was a beautiful, successful businesswoman from Great Britain and I am, well, me: an Indian homemaker and a freelancer.

Growing up her mother ensured that she knew how to make soaps while mine forced me to learn how to sew. Both our mothers belonged to different worlds, the first one, a teacher in a developed nation and the second, a housewife in a small town in a developing nation. Though separated by oceans and economies, the thought behind the actions was the same. We were the daughters, the future wives and guardians of our families. Education was important but we needed something beyond that. We needed a tangible skill that would help us provide for our families if ever needed. A skill that would give our hands the strength to take care of ourselves and our loved ones. The skills that ensured we had the means to earn a living, food on the table, a roof over our head and clothes on our back no matter the circumstances life brings us to.

Being daughters, we resisted. It was beneath us, we were the women of a new independent world, we walked hand in hand with the men and if a man did not need these skills, we definitely had no use for them. It was a battle we heroically fought and lost.

Today, she runs a successful artisan soap and shampoo company and I design wedding apparel. Our moms struggled to give us a skill that was a safety net, instead they laid the foundation stones of our identities.

Mother Earth

The earth whispers. Unfortunately, there are few who possess ears for her. Sometimes it is her groans under the weight of humanity and its ceaseless march towards riches and fame.

At times, she finds herself weeping for the children who have been lost, not just in the literal sense, but for the grand trees that once graced the landscape, the rich lands that bore nourishing fruits, and the innocent creatures that inhabited those spaces. Her tears flow for the sweet sounds of birds' songs and the cries of animals that have been silenced by the relentless noise of factories and heavy machinery. But then, there are moments of joy when she smiles, celebrating simple yet profound experiences like a child's first smile, the kindness shown to a stranger, or the comforting embrace of a friend in distress, all while feeling deep humility and gratitude. The earth witnesses and hears everything that happens, just as we do. However, she carries the weight of it all alone.

During the quiet hours of the night, when everyone around me is peacefully asleep, I occasionally hear her soft voice amidst the soothing sounds of gentle snores, distant traffic, and the tranquil rustle of trees and birds. She expresses no requests or grievances; instead, she simply utters a heartfelt prayer. “May my children thrive,” she softly whispers, “and allow others to do the same.”

Healthy Desserts

It was late evening, and she clutched the grocery bag closer. It was a long walk home–the cold and darkness made it feel even longer. Winters were already cold–did they have to be so dark and foggy too? she thought, brushing aside the scientific explanation.

She didn't hate winters, she reminded herself. She didn't mind the cold, and could tolerate the wetness that crept up from underfoot. Winter was a beautiful season–the blanket of snow, the trees showing off their bones, and the food. The food made everything–

Lost in her inner dialogue, it took her a moment to register the footsteps behind her. They carried a sense of urgency, drawing closer with every step. She turned. The man's nonchalant expression was at odds with his pace, which was quickly closing the distance between them. Her heart pounded. She braced herself for the attack she was almost certain would come.

She was right. The man lunged for her sling bag, ignoring the glaringly bright grocery bag. She tried to push him away, but he was too tall and strong for her to make any impact. He tugged at her arm, and the tiny bag slipped from her fingers.

Without thinking, she swung the grocery bag at him. He smirked—what harm could a bag of fruit and bread possibly do? The bag struck his head. He staggered, took two steps back. Blood trickled from his forehead, and the bag clattered to the pavement. He should have considered the possibility that the grocery bag carried something heavy—and hard enough to hurt him.

It was her turn to smirk. She picked up the bag, brushed off the dirt and wore it across her body. Her impulsive dessert purchase had paid off. Rasgullas are bad for your health, they say!!

Grey

3:00 AM.

The baby's cries wake her from a dreamless sleep.

"How quickly life changes," she thinks, as she hugs the baby close. Just over eighteen months ago, she'd be staggering into her one-room apartment at this hour—heels in one hand, laughter and cigarette smoke still clinging to her hair. Life had felt full: work, friends, parties, love.

Then she decided to kick the relationship into a higher gear.

Things were great. But babies need space, clean air, and somewhere safe to crawl. So they moved—to a cute cottage in an even cuter village, with a white picket fence and ivy climbing the walls. She loved it. A new chapter. A fresh start.

Happiness felt almost within reach: a healthy baby, a husband who loved her, a home worthy of postcards. What more could she ask for?

Only, the husband was always at work—or coming back from it. What little time he had went straight to the baby. Sweet nothings on the pillow became shopping lists on the fridge. Her friends now lived in a different orbit. Calls became rare. Invitations stopped coming. The parties were non- existent

Every morning, she saw a little less of herself in the mirror.

Bit by bit, she was fading—into the soft grey walls of the cottage, into the silence between feedings, into the space between what she'd dreamed and what had come to be.

The Cook

Before you dive in, you need to know - I am a great cook. Ask around if you don't want to believe me. With that out of the way, let's now dive into the tale for the day, the day of disasters in the kitchen.

It was a bright snowy day, and I knew it was special before my feet hit the ground. I took out some pastry dough that had been hiding in the fridge for a couple of days, along with some vegetables and cheese. You guessed it, stuffed puff pastry was the breakfast for the day.

My hands were itching to take out my brand new chopper for a chopp-ty-chop and must say it worked like a spell. In no time I had chopped all the veggies - onions, a bit of carrot, and some cabbage. I used my hands to give it all a gentle massage, a good mix and then layered the veggies with generous amounts of cheese. Tada! In the oven the pastry dough goes. Easy-peasy.

Then I think, why not make cabbage rice? It was the new healthy thing on the block. I did not feel the need to check a recipe or two, this ain't my first rodeo. The new chopper is too small for this, so I take out the bigger one. The chopper chops my cabbage too fine and needless to say I have a Greek tragedy in my hands.

Somehow, I grab the chopper blades wrong and get a taste of their sharp edge.

In the oven there's another nasty surprise unfolding; the strong smell of burnt veggies and dough that reaches my nose. I was too generous with my vegetables and cheese and the dough fails to rise. The stuffed puff pastry is both raw and burnt at the same time.

My daughter goes smiling to school with bread and butter along with a huge slice of cake and my husband can't stop laughing. I learn a lesson, no matter what I put on the table from the kitchen, I am a genius born to save the day!!

Not a love Letter: 01

This is not a love letter. I don't think writing a love letter to a girl on the eve before her wedding is cool, and you know me, I am anything but cool. That said, I know that you are aware that I do love you.

No, I do not want to marry you, I concur when you proudly state that you will be a poor example of a wife. You do not like to lead and hate following others, you hate looking after others and cry when they exhibit independence. You love cooking and get bored with making meals. Being with you 24 X 7 will drive me crazy in a week and you in just twenty-four hours.

That explained, I do not exactly know how to define my love for you. It is not romantic, nor the love siblings share. I do not hero worship you - you have not done anything hero worship worthy, except laugh at all my jokes, some lame ones even, in the six months I have known you. You have all the qualities that make a human humane. You are kind, funny, intelligent, decent looking, articulate and can even count. But so was my ex-girlfriend, and I do not think I love her anymore.

And, at the other end of the spectrum, you stand. We are the best of friends now. Like you claim to know me,

I too, know a lot about you and what goes on in that crazy head. Three years from now you will remember me but struggle to remember my name. Then maybe you turn back to get a second look when we cross a street a decade later, and finally, I will be a distant warm memory in your heart. A fleeting thought that will make you smile on the chilliest days.

Let us call this love we share 'incomplete love'. We could have been the almost lovers who parted ways after a bitter fight, or best friends who live and grow old side by side. Or maybe neighbours who share much more than a common fence. Possibilities are endless, but nothing would come from it, for we share nothing but this incomplete, undefinable love.

******

This is not a love letter", his letter started. He was my best friend. For whole six months, mid August to the end of January. We worked together, ate our meals together and roamed around the dusty roads of Delhi together. He was my best friend in the true sense. He listened when I bitched about our boss and agreed when I declared we had the best boss ever. He drove me to meet my boyfriend and even offered to pick me up.

Then out of the blue, just as I was leaving for home after my last day at work, he gave me the letter. I had invited him to my wedding , but he never came. I was not surprized. Life happened and we lost touch. Honestly, that "not a love letter" was our last conversation. Today he is a faint memory that keeps getting fainter in the harsh light of the sun. But a memory that always makes me smile.

Be happy dear friend, wherever you are. I sure hope your days of trying to light up petrol tanks are now over.

Not a love letter :02

Dear Uncle and Aunty,

Thanks for lunch yesterday. I enjoyed both the company and the food. It was great to meet people so passionate about food and movies. You might have just convinced me that Dev Anand was a far better actor than my favourite Shahrukh. I am still not a fan of red shirts though.

In the fun conversation that flowed easily, I did not forget the purpose of our meeting. It was an opportunity for you to get to know the girl who might soon be a part of your family a little better.

"How do I feel about Raj?" I know this was the question you wanted to ask but were too polite to. Raj, he is handsome and smart and loving and articulate. The thought of him makes my tummy flutter and steals away my breath. Is this love? Maybe, I am not sure. He makes me feel something I have never felt before–happy, light, free. Though I have worked in hotels and restaurants for years, I had never tried so many new foods and cuisines before meeting Raj. He always knows what I would like even before I do.

And now to the part you will not like.

The truth is, Raj is not the only man I am seeing, I am also meeting Jai. Jai is diametrically opposite to Raj. While Raj lives in the moment, Jai's life is planned down to the minute. I suspect he already has a date for his nuptials. As you might have guessed, he also, approached me through the marriage bureau. The intention was also the same; we meet over a couple of months and decide if we would like to get married. It has been six months, and both Raj and Jai are mulling over the decision while I wait.

Raj, the (uncrowned) prince of a large estate and numerous businesses, looks for a future princess in me. Someone who is beautiful, kind and able to stand beside him through thick and thin. A wife who would accompany him to parties and social events and cheer from the sidelines as he takes the business and the family wealth to new heights.

Jai, an army pilot, too looks for a wife, an army wife. Someone who does not mind getting her hands dirty whether while managing his household, host parties and lunches for his battalion and participate enthusiastically in the duties of an army wife.

You know the funny thing? Neither of them ever question what I want. Do I desire to be the beloved princess or the revered army wife ? The question was if I fit the future they envision for themselves and their families, not the future I desire. They seem disinterested in the dreams of the orphan girl who works as a manager in an uptown restaurant. A home, a loving husband and a stable life, what more could I want? I agreed, and then I met you.

Yesterday, I got an opportunity to observe you as a couple. Aunty, you are the wife and the queen, and yet I saw you too. Your identity and your opinions are not just a reflection of your husband's point of view, they are your beliefs and experiences too. I saw you disagree. Both of you held on to your beliefs, without the need to pull the other down. Your husband is a successful businessman and you are an acclaimed professor. You stand by your husband as much as he stands by you. You walk down the path, hand in hand, sometimes uncle takes the lead and sometimes you but always as partners and equals.

I covet that – a relationship between equals. So today I met both Raj and Jai and told them that I was moving on. They will have to look for a life partner elsewhere. My only hope is that I can keep meeting you once in a while.

Regards
Preeti.

Love's Labour Lost: 01

Kirti.

It was something small that reminded him of Kirti. Something that most of us miss, something insignificant that you notice disappearing from the corner of your eye. The way the stranger walked or her bright silver jacket with faux fur or maybe, her joyous laughter that floated across the street. It had been over six months since they talked or even exchanged messages. That may not be a big thing for most of his friends, but six months of radio silence was monumental when it came to Kirti.

His mind went to the message she sent him on the eve of his departure. The message claimed - he was her best friend, confidant and partner in crime. Her 'Kokoro no tomo'- the friend of her soul. Distance did not make the heart grow fonder. There was a time when he was a part of every decision she made, and today he learnt about her engagement to a guy he knew only through social networking sites.

The shift was gradual: like a slow-moving glacier. He did not even notice when the frequent calls morphed into messages and then to likes and hearts on Facebook. The journey from an active participant in her life to a mute spectator standing on the sidelines was now complete. Maybe things would have turned out differently if he had professed his feelings for her. But that evening was earmarked for goodbyes and promises to stay in touch forever. He did visit her a few times, but each time was a little worse than last. Her kindness, her concern, and her smile were all there – he was just removed from it all – like a moon orbiting his earth- always falling towards her but never quite reaching.

His hand trembled slightly over her picture. She was smiling as brightly as ever surrounded by new friends and family, people he had never met. The thing that hurt the most was that they were in the restaurant that was once theirs. "A place to get away from it all," she said.

It was time to move on; she had apparently done that already.

Pawan.

She loved him, more than anyone could ever fathom. That day, on the eve of his departure she was sure he would say something, instead, he handed her the Polaroid camera. She needed to simply close her eyes to see the picture. Him and his lopsided grin with an arm around another friend.

They did not promise to stay in touch, theirs was a relationship beyond the physics of distances. How naïve had she been! First, it was the different time zones and then the new job. Gradually, the phone calls became WhatsApp messages. It is impossible to replace a phone call that ended with one of them falling asleep with text messages. No matter what she felt, something was missing from their conversations. She loved him because he understood her silences. How does one convey those pauses, that silence over a text. She waited for him to read her silence again. As the silences grew longer, he became distant, and she lost her patience.

Two years. That was the time she waited for him to come back to her, but he never did. She was now exhausted from the wait. Maybe, when life pushed them on different paths, he continued walking while, she stood waiting from him at the same corner. Maybe, his path would never bring him to her. She pulled out the picture to keep it on the sidewalk. He had found his path and it was finally time to say goodbye.

Love's labour lost - the story that never began.

Love's Labour Lost: 02

Click- load - comment.

Ravi was familiar with their routine. He clicked the picture, loaded it and waited for Saana to respond. It was chicken with pasta - something she would have loved had she accompanied him on the trip. As he expected, his mobile pinged almost instantly. "Not even five minutes" he smiled, "Saana did not disappoint."

Ravi was disappointed. It was a like and comment from Reem. "Look who is eating green chicken now" the comment read. It referred to a conversation decades ago, when Ravi claimed he did not and would never eat green-coloured food. The comment and the fact that the picture was meant for Saana and not Reem, irritated Ravi.

Reem was a good friend in another lifetime. They were never romantically involved. Reem knew the real him, the one he kept hidden under layers of a carefully crafted social persona . To be honest, Ravi did once contemplate spending the rest of his life with her. Time passed, they grew older, and with them, their relationship evolved. He discovered Reem was controlling in numerous little ways. Like how she was supportive of Ravi, however, only when she agreed, and at times she was unreasonably critical. There were decisions she made in her life, choices Ravi did not agree with, but he believed a friend's job was unquestioning support. He made it a point to be there for her, his opinions carefully tucked away. With time the relationship made Ravi feel trapped.

Life took them on different paths, and he hoped like many friends and acquaintances, they too would painlessly drift away. That did not happen – the more he drifted away the more forceful Reem became. She demanded more of his time, questioned his every move and had an opinion on every aspect of his life - from the new shirt he bought, to the project he signed up for at work and even his Bumble profile. Reem was aware of where she stood in Ravi's life. It was a special place, loved and cherished. For some reason she chose to ignore the boundaries and crawl deeper into Ravi's life. Personal, professional, physical and emotional she demanded to be there with her suggestions and strong opinions. She succeeded in breaking his heart and pushing herself out.

His thumb hovered over the heart icon, the cursor of his mind stuck between gratitude and irritation. He could almost hear the text notification that would follow if he tapped the emoticon. The memory of how Reem invited herself to a trip to Shimla on the mere mention of an office trip floated to the top of his head.

The fact that Saana and Ravi were in a relationship or that was work did not seem to matter to Reem. Ravi still loved Reem in his special way. She had taught him a lot and was there for him when things got tough. He was eternally grateful.

The relationship that they once shared and enjoyed was long over. Ravi knew that and there were enough signs for Reem to realize the truth. Maybe, it was his fault that Reem was unaware. She was hanging on to the last fragile thread of their relationship and Ravi was the one who needed to cut it off. "You are a coward," Reem joked often. She was right. He didn't want to be the one to break her heart.

Heaving a heavy sigh, though Ravi's thumb still hovered, he didn't press the heart.

Still Yours

There you were, sitting across the room with a drink in your hand. The room was poorly lit, crowded, and music blared from the speakers placed strategically around. Through it all, it took me only a millisecond to find you. I said a million times that I would always find my way back to you. It was you who didn't believe me.

You moved on.

All those promises–to never forget me, to always be by my side, to walk beside me... forgotten. Just like your wine glass, left behind on the table, as the lady in the tight dress leads you to the dance floor. I have some choice words for your dance partner, but I shall refrain. I never liked curse words.

Your voice is animated, your eyes shine as the woman leans in closer to hear what you're saying. The fact that her hand rests on your arm, and you make no attempt to escape her clutches, does not escape my notice.

You look handsome, and a happy glow warms your face– just like it did the night you professed your love for me.

I was naive. Hopelessly in love. I thought that look, that smile, was mine forever.

That I would be the only one you'd ever hold in your arms. I was wrong.

Today, you have moved on.

It didn't hurt to see that you had moved on. What broke me was the moment our eyes met across the room– and you looked right through me.

I guess death did do us part.

Roots

The tree was old and rotting inside. For decades, it had provided shade, fruit, and oxygen—but now, it posed a danger and had to be removed.

The village elders needed a new place to hold the panchayat. The men required a new spot for their evening hookah and games of cards. They expected some debate about the replacement site. There was none. Everyone quickly agreed to the spot suggested by the panch. His position warranted respect, and agreeing with him was a good way to show it.

"What of the wood?" asked a young man sitting at the back. He was a carpenter—perhaps he saw purpose where others saw only decay. Even in death, the great tree still held value.

"Yes, the trunk may be rotten," added a man sitting in the corner, "but it will make excellent firewood."

The discussion stirred another man awake. He had been napping through most of the meeting, but the mention of wood had piqued his interest—there was money to be made.

"It belongs to us," declared a middle-aged man, rising to his feet. "My wife's great-great-grandfather planted it."

"Then it surely belongs to us," said a woman, pulling her husband's arm. "It was my husband's great-great-grandfather."

The panch tried to interrupt, but before he could speak, another woman raised her voice.

"Planting is not enough," she said. "Our clan tended that tree for generations. It's our men who'll take the risk of cutting it down. That's payment enough. The wood is ours."

"As if you need more money," the village priest snapped. "You and your clan are greedy. We worshipped that tree for years. The wood is our prasad."

The village headmaster cleared his throat. He had hoped to use the wood to build benches or mend the broken fence. But he knew his voice—no matter how loud—would not be heard.

A man stood up at the edge of the gathering. His voice was calm, but carried weight. He owed the biggest land parcel in the village. "The tree grows beside my field. For generations, everyone's cut through my crops to reach it. No one ever offered compensation. And now that there's money to be made from this wretched tree, everyone lays claim. It belongs to no one—but me and my sons."

The panch closed his eyes as the voices rose around him. Soon, the words blurred into a deafening roar that drowned all reason, all compassion, all memory of the tree's true worth. He stood, retied his turban, and walked away.

It was a battle he had to fight– but today was not the day.

The Gardner

Dearest Gulabo,

I know you hate the name. Blame our parents - they were the ones to name you Rohini, the pretty rose.

That said, remember the proverbs we learnt in Hindi language class?

It's been three weeks, and my plants survive. Well, I presume they do. The plants die at a much slower pace than animals I believe. Or maybe they let go of life a small inch by inch hoping to turn back any moment, fighting till the last possible minute. I reckon it is that - The flowers in a vase survive for days after being brutally separated from the plant. Filling our homes with heavenly fragrance and making them look gorgeous. Almost like all the houses in the architectural magazines you hoard. Good Homes, right?

But let's be real, if my plants had feelings, they'd probably be plotting a revenge heist to escape their ceramic prisons while I'm busy googling "how to keep a cactus alive." So, if you happen to find a tiny plant army gathering in the corner of my living room, just know they're not planning a coup, but rather a desperate bid for freedom–probably led by the most dramatic fern, complete with a tiny banner that reads, “We want soil, not pot!”

I digress, my plants live. Today I took a pair of scissors to my rose plant chopping off the drying leaves and stem. There are two green nodes left full of promise of new leaves and possibly a rose or two. The other two are okay. But as we have seen in the past, plants have a way of drying out and dying on me. I water them every day- but there is always too much or too little water. You were the one who pointed out that I drowned my mint plant with my morning watering routine. I have bought a spray bottle now – It is cute - pink with a small bow on the top. Hopefully, my three remaining plants are not drowning anymore.

To be named Champakali, the fragrant flower and have a black thumb like mine, what irony! What was the proverb for this? Something about having qualities opposite to your name. It sounds much better in Hindi I bet. I remember we learnt it and a hundred more. Remind me.

Do you think I should get some pet fish? It will be difficult, almost impossible to drown them.

Love.
Your sister,
Champakali.

Quiet Exit

Drinks, background music, and gossip. The dancing was done, and people had drifted into the quiet corners. Stories began to spill—light at first, then deeper. As always, the conversation turned to exes and the shattered pieces they left behind. They shared their heartbreaks. I stayed quiet, watching the warmth of my hands melt the ice in my drink. I had nothing to offer.

I was the one who walked away—leaving behind tears, pleas, and a broken heart.

I'm not sure when or how I made that decision. The reasons blur in hindsight. But through the maze of emotions and consequences, one truth stands out: walking away was the best thing I could have done. For her. For me. I can almost feel her smirk even now. She still possessed the power to send a chill down my spine.

Every relationship leaves behind a few good memories. I saw that around me—smiles shining through the tears. The kind of memories that sneak up on you in the middle of a cold night, warming you as you pull the blanket tighter.

Mine are different.

I remember the moment the pedestal I'd placed her on crumbled. I remember realising that love, no matter how deep, isn't always enough. I remember holding onto silence while she cried, begged for an explanation, pleaded to understand.

I saw her pain. I saw her point of view. I tried. But I couldn't make myself feel what she needed me to.

I didn't leave because I stopped loving her. I didn't leave for someone else.

I left because she wanted more than I could give. I left because she didn't want to love me—she wanted to own me.

Respect for Respect

The challenge wasn't holding back the tears that threatened to spill or resisting the urge to simply get up and leave the room. Surprisingly, sitting there with a fixed smile, staring at a TV screen spewing content that could lower anyone's IQ, was easy.

All she wanted was his opinion. He was a smart man—one didn't get to his level without intelligence, hard work, and street smartness. He was the one who had explained why working from the office mattered long before content creators had found the topic. Lunch was done, and they were all gathered around the TV. Banter and conversation flowed effortlessly, as it often did, when the question formed in her mind.

She didn't expect him to agree with her; after all, she was just a housewife, and he a Senior VP in a multinational corporation. But she hoped he would expand her thinking, help her see the issue from a different perspective. She loved talking to people she considered more accomplished and who by virtue of their experience were more knowledgeable than her. These conversations, no matter the direction they took, always left her feeling enriched, like she'd gained another new lens through which to view the world.

What she didn't expect was to be shut down so quickly–or so brutally. He didn't even let her finish. The irritation in his voice, the stern expression on his face, and the way his back stiffened as he continued to stare at the TV, refusing to meet her gaze, said it all. His body language screamed louder than words: *"You and your ideas are stupid. Don't waste my time."*

She had been put back in her place–reminded of her unspoken role as the younger sister, the wife, the mother. A person who was meant to fade into the background. A person who, though not literally chained to the stove in the kitchen, certainly existed that way in the minds of those around her. Accepting that truth wasn't easy, but it was a fact of life for her.

What was impossible, though, was the realisation that, while he might return her love and care for her in his own way, he did not respect her.

Missing Home

It was a long line that was slowly inching forward. I felt tired, hungry, and a bit anxious. Men in uniforms and positions of authority intimidate me. When the immigration officer asked for the purpose of our visit, I feebly replied, "We are going home."

The word 'home' is one I instinctively use to describe the place and country I have been living in for less than eight months, which is only about 2% of my lifetime. It's not just the word choice; I started to miss 'home' after being away for just three days. It's ironic considering that I don't speak the language of my 'home' and spend hours in the kitchen trying to recreate the flavours from 'back' home. After years of exclusively watching English movies and TV shows, I've started to watch Hindi films just to feel a connection to the home I left behind. I turn around to look at the person whenever I hear a familiar accent, hoping to catch a glimpse of someone who might share my sense of nostalgia. My favourite spot in the public park is under the tree that almost looks like the one in my old school.

Honestly, I don't know what defines home for me anymore. Is it where I currently live or where I grew up and have family? Is it the land that holds memories of the past, or the one where I am creating memories for the future? No matter which side of the ocean I'm on, I'm always missing home.

Perhaps this is the expat lifestyle—the peculiar luxury of missing home even while you are at home!

Two of a Kind

The rhythmic clank and bang of the train wheels, the fast-moving scenery, a steaming cup of tea—and conversations that always start somewhere and end up somewhere else.

"Who's your favourite God?" A question pops up.

"Favourite God?" There's a pause. "God is an eternal being who looks over us. God is above our concepts of gender, race, identity, and names."

"Ahaa!" A smile—genuine and free of sarcasm or mockery. "A Hindu with a Christian ideology!

My favourite God is Ganesh, the elephant god," the conversation continues. "Raised by a single mother and punished ruthlessly for trying to protect her honour—not by an angry mob or a self-righteous protector of societal values, but by his own father!

Can you imagine the ridicule he would have faced in school? A short and fat kid, no father in sight, and when 'father dearest' does make an appearance, our young god ends up being the only kid with an elephant head.

My heart goes out to the young Ganesh—the boy before the god."

"Ahaa!" The smile is returned—warm and affectionate. "A traditionalist with modern values. We're two of a kind."

A Brother's Sacrifice

"What you ask for dear husband, is much more than sacrificing the comforts of the palace, and the life of a princess." She gingerly touched the red bangles on her wrist. They felt heavy and unfamiliar. " You accompany Lord Ram and Sister Sita to fulfil your duties as a brother yet, you keep me from following my sister. You tell me not to follow you, my husband."

She paused, waiting for a response that did not come. "Sleep for fourteen years, you say. Fourteen years of my life, lost in a single moonless night. And with it, I lose the tears of watching my husband part from me; the comfort of my family, my parents, I lose their blessings and their love. Fourteen springs, fourteen summers, and fourteen winters, all invisible to my unfeeling sleeping eyes."

"I grew up in the shadow of my sister, Sita. I played with her, laughed and cried with her and then married her husband's brother, hoping to be with her forever. Today, you sever that bond. I always walked holding her hand, today you leave me without support, without guidance and without any idea where to go." Tears spilled over, yet she did not wipe them. Her voice remained steady, her back straight. The wedding finery weighed on her, but she bore it with strength.

"I married you with a promise to be your partner, in happiness and sadness, and your vow robs me of the opportunity to walk with you." She took a deep breath before continuing. The urge to shout at him was strong. "I shall not sit on the window, counting days for your return." She did not allow her voice to betray the anger, the helplessness and the fear she felt. "I cannot shed tears or suffer the pain of separation. Should the need arise, I cannot follow Lord Yama to fight for your life, nor fast for your victories. I shall be asleep, oblivious to your struggles, your pain, and your victories."

"You follow Ram, on the path to become an immortal, a God. While I stay back here, stripped of my rightful place in history, reduced to the one who married Lakshman."

Lakshman stood there, in stoic silence. His eyes brimming, tears threatening to roll down as he faced his bride, the young, dreamy-eyed girl who sat beside him during the wedding rituals. The innocent girl who looked towards her sister for approval and encouragement during the journey home. The girl who had metamorphized into a woman right in front of his eyes. He knew he asked for a great sacrifice. He struggled to find an answer, to somehow soothe the burning pain she felt, but words failed him. He took a tentative step forward, hoping to embrace her, and convey the guilt he was burdened with. Maybe wipe her tears and create a memory they could hold on to, on cold, unforgiving nights that would follow.

“Go, my husband, say your goodbyes." She took a step back, away from his half stretched arms." I shall prepare for the long night and the silence ahead." She swiftly turned and went into her bedchamber without a backward glance.

Waiting for My Drona

"I am Eklavya, patiently waiting for my Drona."

"Why Drona?" The response to the statement was a question.

"Who else but Drona?" It was a relaxed conversation, flowing freely—without judgment or the pressure of a timetable.

"The teacher who inspired generations. The guide who led archers, wrestlers, mace-bearers, and kings on the path of glory. They may have been mortal, yet they live on in our memories, in our literature, and on our screens. He was the warrior before whom even the mighty Pandavas almost bent their knees. The father who challenged fate for his son—and won. Who else but Drona?"

"Why Eklavya then? Not Arjuna or even Karna?"

"The forest youth. The outsider. The one with a lowly birth who mastered the art better than the students who learned it. The student who gave up his future—willingly—to appease his teacher. Not a tear spilled for the pain he must have felt as blood sprouted from the place where his thumb once was. The proud warrior who stood against the army of a God. Nameless, rank-less, a foot soldier relegated to the footnotes of history.

History, my friend, is not kind to the losing side—but that does not mean we fail to recognize the greatness that was."

Mahatma to Mortal

His death was a shock. Heartfelt speeches were made. Quotes repeated. Grief echoed across the land. Millions flocked to see their beloved Mahatma—some for a final farewell, others believing that touching his feet would open the gates of heaven. A few refused to believe the news until they saw it with their own eyes. The outpouring of pain, tears, and despair seemed destined to elevate the man to the status of a god. He had done much—for his people, his country, and the world.

"Judgement and criticism," he often joked, "are my best friends." He was a leader, but his followers were not sheep. They questioned him, challenged him, and in doing so, kept him honest. He made mistakes, and he owned them. Sometimes with a careless laugh and at times after a long debates. But one thing was certain: he had vision. He saw farther than most. His love for his people and his land was unquestionable. Not everyone liked him, not everyone agreed with him—but they all followed him willingly.

Time passed. Decades rolled by and both life and the nation moved on.

Seven decades later, his name is still remembered—his charisma, his ideals, the enormous influence he once held. He is still considered a leader, but now with fewer followers. His life is examined under harsher lights. His words are scrutinized. His legacy, revised. The journey from Mahatma to flawed mortal has begun—only, he is no longer here to defend, to explain, or to grow.

His statue still stands in the city square—untouched, garlanded on national days, but rarely looked in the eye

God and Saviour

"Sita!"

The thunder in Ravana's voice sent the maids scurrying in all directions. "This is your last chance. Submit to being my wife, and I shall let Ram and his army of monkeys go back unharmed."

"No, mighty king, that shall never happen. Let the world see the mighty king fall on the feet of the poor prince and his army of monkeys." Sita continued making the flower garland, refusing to stand-up and give Ravana the respect he demanded as the king.

"So, this is nothing more than an evil king abducting the poor helpless princess and the warrior prince coming to her rescue."

"Then what do you think all this is?" Sita looked up, meeting Ravana's gaze. "Why would Ram come here with his army?"

Ravana stepped closer and lowered his voice, "You think I am unaware of what happens here. You need to get off the high horse, young princess. You talk about Ram defending your honour when you choose to stay here. No, no save that false indigitation." He continued, "You did not accept me, nor escape back to your precious Ram when you had the opportunity. You, my dear princess, made a choice to let this war happen, not once but twice."

"You—you do not know what you are talking about" Sita stammered. The incomplete garland slipped off her fingers.

"Not so comfortable now, are you?" Ravana guffawed. "Yes, I know all about the offer Hanuman made to you to take you back with him. Yet, you sat here, watching the war unfold. You let blood paint the battleground red. Hundreds die every day, husbands, brothers, and young sons while you weave garlands to welcome your saviour.

"You do not understand," she whispered hoarsely.

"Then explain, if you can." Ravana unsuccessfully tried to keep the anguish from his voice. He had lost too much in this war. It would be a hollow victory if there was one. "Go on princess. Tell me why you sit here, in this quiet garden, watching the world burn down around you? They tell me you are a Goddess. One without mercy I add. Should you choose, you could walk out anytime—a garden guarded by four women who fear me but worship you. A post-dinner walk, and you could be in the arms of your loving prince long before any one of your guards raise the alarm. He stepped a closer to her. "Tell me, why Sita?

It was a long while before Sita lifted her head from her hands. Her voice, barely audible, carried the weight of truth. "You are right. Every word you say is true. I do not need to be rescued." She took a steadying breath, her fingers deftly returning to the garland. Then, her voice grew stronger, each word sharpened with conviction. "I am not a damsel in distress, not for a moment. But Ram—my Ram—needs to rescue his honour and his name."

Honour Lost

A thin fabric falls off my shoulder, and all honour is lost before the cloth touches the ground: mine, that of my parents, my husbands, my kingdom, my clan and maybe even the Gods I worship. All is lost, yet not a muscle moves; a few drops of moisture roll down on a cheek. I stand there, broken, defeated and humiliated.

I am no ordinary woman; I am the one born of fire, the wife of the greatest warriors on earth, the empress of the nation, and the sister of the mightiest God, and yet, other than a feeble curse that falls off my lips, I have nothing to avenge my honour.

I turn to my father; if my honour was attached to my clothes and hair, why can't I be the one to protect it? My husbands, who vowed to love and protect me, your dharma kept you from lifting your bow or your mace; what kept you from rolling a weapon in my direction? The God, the great one who promised to pay the debt in my hour of need, you too, failed me. Yet the story gets told again and again. It is the tale of the victory of truth over falsehood, right over wrong and good over evil! It is not the tale of a woman losing and regaining her honour. I am sometimes the damsel in distress and sometimes the cause of the greatest battle. I am the one who lost her honour and the one whose hands are red with the blood of innocents.

No one sees me; no one notices my hands tied behind my back. I am nothing but a pawn moved from one square to another as the grand saga unfolds. Surrounded by friends and family always, yet, forever alone.

My daughters in the future who listen to my tale on their grandmother's lap, read about me in books, or perhaps discuss my contribution to the great epic: Remember this – your honour is yours to keep and to defend. You are the queen, the king in the game of chess that is your life. So step up and take charge.

Not My Sons

"Stop"

It was not the command but the voice that made everyone freeze. All those years, she sat there, three paces behind her husband, the king, occasionally nodding to the proceeding in the court of the great nation. If she had a voice, no one heard it, she was blessed with sight, but everyone knew she had given it up for her beloved husband.

She stood up to walk to her younger son, angrily waving away the aide who stepped forward to help her. His cruel laughter from a moment ago was enough to reach him. She held out her hand. There was no doubt he knew what she was asking for.

"Mother, you –"

Her expression cut short his justification. She took the sari and followed it to its defeated owner. The owner was a queen a short while ago, and now they said she was a slave.

"Queen mother, you mustn't" The wise minister spoke up. He was the one well versed with the rules and laws, even the king came to him for counsel.

She draped the sari across the woman's bare shoulders and held on as she cried. Finally, when the violent sobs quietened down, she turned towards the exit.

"You can't" the minister added "Queen Mother" a pause later. "It is against the laws of men."

"Exactly, wise minister" she paused, but did not bother turning to face him. " The laws of men state that this disgraceful scene that unfolded here was fair. That my sons and their cousins are following their dharma. You, your king, the elders in the court are all bound by these inflexible laws made by men. But you forget, o' wise minister, I am not a man. Hence, laws of men do not bind me.

"Mother" the voice of her eldest son boomed across the courtroom. She felt the poor woman tremble beneath the thin fabric of the sari.

Her silence encouraged him, he knew he was her favourite and she would always do what he asked for. After all, she was his mother and he was the firstborn son.

"All this has been too much for you" he continued, softening his voice to disguise his anger. He motioned the aides to help her. "Perhaps, you should retire to your chambers."

This time, she turned to the sound of his voice. Tucking the woman behind her, she pushed away the aide who gently touched her elbow.

"Mother?" she replied. She did not raise her voice, nor did she make any attempt to hide her contempt. Her voice was clear and calm as it rang across the great hall. "I did not raise a son who could disrespect women. I raised a man who was kind, a just ruler, great statesman, a man people could look up to. You are merely a reflection of the values I tried to instilled in you. He is young he will learn, I kept telling myself. But today, you have chosen to turn away from the very principles that define true nobility. You may be the prince, even the future king, but your brothers and are not my worthy of being called my sons," declared.

The Glorious End

So, this is how it ends. I die knee-deep in mud and an arrow pierced through my back. Not a glorious end a warrior like me desires, but I seek solace in the fact that Arjun did not get a magnificent victory either. I doubt anyone will know him as 'Mighty Arjun, the slayer of Karna.' My defeat was the end of a tragic life, not a celebrated moment in Arjun's saga. My name shall always be a question mark on his claim as a righteous warrior, the best archer in the world. Through the pain and humiliation, there is a small reason to smile.

Maybe I deserved this end. To be honest, I deserve worst. My ego, my role in the disrobing of Devi Draupadi in the court, and the death of son Abhimanyu. No matter what I do or did, I can't get rid of the shadow of these vile acts. I know I will walk into the inextinguishable fires of hell, and I do not flinch. Perhaps in those flames of guilt and remorse, I may finally begin to atone.As I make way to my pyre, I pray these are not the only two moments that define me. I do not desire to be known for my generosity- those were only feeble attempts at redemption.

I am not and will never be a Pandava. I am a Kuntiya. I will not deny my Ma Kunti her motherhood, even though she was never a mother to me. To her I was never her son, just her mark of shame. Aloof from her other sons, my brothers, I stand alone. I am a warrior, but not the one on the winning side. In this battle of good over evil, I am not the one fighting for the good. All warriors wish for victories and ballads, and I am no exception. But I know that ballads are not written about the fallen.

I know that Duryodhana and his brothers would eventually make it to the heaven for they met Lord Yama with weapons in their hands. While here I am, unarmed, knee deep in mud as Lord Yama comes to collect my soul. The gates of heaven will not open for me.

If there were one thing I hope progeny remembers me for, it would be my loyalty. I stood behind my friend, Duryodhana, through it all. I stood one step behind my friend, unwavering in my support while his family, friends and even his beloved Gods left his side. It was Duryodhana who bestowed me a crown and the title of a friend. I repaid that debt with my family ties, my life and my values and beliefs. My soul burns in the fires of hell, waiting for another humble birth for another chance at heaven. I do not crave for the glory of a warrior, but Karana, the loyal friend, does have a beautiful ring to it.

Mother

"Mother!! You cannot abandon us."

She intended to walk away, but the pain in the voice melted her resolve like a sole snowflake under a harsh summer sun.

"I do not abandon you, my sons. I leave you in the skilful hands of your father, his loyal brother, under the roof of your forefathers and kingdom."

"But you walk away. How can a family be complete without a mother, is the home of my forefathers not your home too? If I am the future king, aren't you the queen? Do your steps not take you further away from your family and your Dharma?"

"Today, My Dharma is now complete , my love. I walk away with heavy steps, but I carry no burden on my shoulders."

"What is our dharma?" Cried a shy voice. She never said it, but he was her favourite. She saw pieces of herself in him. His twin was more like their father; first, to take action, he on the other hand, took a moment to consider the consequences before drawing his sword.

"Dharma? What do I know of Dharma? All my life, I walked on the path of Dharma, and the path brings me here today. A mother without sons, an abandoned wife, an exiled queen and a forgotten daughter.

Follow the path of a daughter, my father said, and I followed my husband to the life of a hermit. You are a wife, protect the family honour, and I rejected luxury and a life of comfort waiting for my husband to rescue me. The Dharma of a queen required I walked through fire without a word of protest. My husband and kingdom cast me aside, yet I followed my Dharma and raised future kings and protectors for them. Today, I follow a mother's Dharma as I reunite my sons with their father and the family.

I never strayed from the path of Dharma, yet today I stand here, alone, empty-handed and with bloody feet. I have nothing left to give!"

"Give us a blessing then", come the united voices she would never hear again.

"I pray for a happy life for you, a path that does not make you Gods, for that path is painful and lonely." She turned and walked on an undefined, obscure path, unpaved by family, kingdom or Dharma.

The route from Sita, the Goddess, to Sita, the woman.

A Garland for Karana

With Arjun gone in the Lakshagraha fire, I see no point in the Swayamvar, and yet I stand here in red and gold. The handmaids say I look like an apsara. I see no reason to believe them, or not believe them. How I look today is of no consequence. What matters is who takes the garland I hold in my hands. It was easier before- I was to be the great Arjun's bride. But now?

My eyes search the great hall and settle on a self-assured prince. Our eyes meet from across the large arena. He bows his head and looks away politely, but I feel weak and powerless to remove my gaze from his glowing visage. I feel I can see his soul through his eyes, and I know that he saw ME, not the princess, nor the fire-born beauty, nor the promise of a king's army. I continue observing him from behind my veil. He carries himself with the confidence of an accomplished warrior as he walks up to the centre of the arena. He bows to the assembly and reaches to lift the bow. There is some commotion behind me but I have eyes only for the warrior whom I see walking towards me. In that fraction of the second my mind weaves a happy future. Images of my varmala, the garland across his broad chest and his strong arms holding me. With Arjun no longer in the picture, wasn't I free to choose my groom? Wouldn't my father be stronger with such a warrior by his side? Our eyes lock again, and this time he holds my gaze, soft yet confident. I feel a thousand butterflies in my stomach. It is an enormous effort not to rush down the distance separating us and place the garland around his neck. He pauses and looks behind him before picking up the bow. It is Duryodhana smiling encouragingly at my warrior. Something about the smile makes me nervous. I look at brother Dhrishtadyumn for reassurance. He stands tense, with a hand on his sword. My father seems worried, all colour drained off his face. Karna! A son of a charioteer, a warrior cursed by his guru Parasurama My warrior is Karna!

" O' great warrior, before you attempt to win my hand in marriage, may I know about the dynasty you hail from?" My voice was strong and bounced off the walls of the arena. This time Karna's actions were slow and deliberate. As he looked at me I saw my infinite love and dreams burn and die in his cold eyes. I take a deep breath to push my tears back and continue.

Mothers of Krishna

Yashoda: He looks so grown up now. I no longer see my little boy in him.

Devaki: He is there. A son never really grows up for his mother.

Yashoda: No – my son was a maakhanchor, a butter stealing cowherd. He spent his days basking in the sun with his cows, playing his mellifluous flute. Your son, Ma Devaki, is the king and future God.

Devaki: You are right. As much as I try – I can't see the carefree cowherd in him. He smiles, yet the smile rarely reaches his eyes. His flute is still his constant companion, yet no one hears the sweet notes anymore. And do you see the weight he carries on his shoulders?

Yashoda: It is so conspicuous, one can't ignore it. I miss his carefree smiles and the sparkle in his eyes. No matter how his day went, he always fell asleep in my arms, playing with my hair.

Devaki: I only hugged him when I saw him, he returned it warmly. But that was it. You had him to yourself – I share him with the world.

Yashoda: I always knew he was on loan. He was mine for a little while. I knew he would go one day, but never imagined he would leave so suddenly, and never look back.

Devaki: You kept a chunk of him in your heart - his childhood! I think it was right in a way- he would lose it here. The world is a cruel place mother, even for our Krishna. You have his innocence mother, hold it tightly in your hand and never it let go.

Yashoda: We are two sides of the same coin, each coveting what the other has and yet never really see the other.

The Cost of Victory

O Lord, what did you do, Krishna? When did you gather this malice, this venom? This insatiable desire to win at all costs. You and I were humble cowherds, happy and content with our cows. When did you see a cow give anything but life-giving nectar?

Where is the honour in defeating a beaten man – a lone man, no longer a king, no longer the leader of the greatest army, a man without his friend, the great warrior Karna? You defeated a tired, beaten man, Krishna, and that too, through duplicitous means. What victory is that, Krishna? Wiping out an entire dynasty?

You say you are establishing a vast empire- the golden age. But look at your foundation – lies, deceit, pain and tears. A foundation lacking values, honesty, compassion and forgiveness. You hope to reap wheat when you sow nothing but datura (poison) seeds. I fear the future; it cannot bring happiness for us.

I am taking my plough. I hope to plant a few seeds of compassion, love, and honour and undo some of the inexcusable behaviour we have displayed in the last 18 days. I hope I accomplish something before fate catches up with us. As we part, I want to give you blessings my younger brother, but my satchel is empty. This battle took away much more than you realize. I will pray for you brother, and your victors – may you all find some peace eventually.

Bound by Dharma

The arrow left the bow, and a strong gust of wind struck my face. In the moment it found its mark, my world tilted. Try as I might, it would never be straight again.

They said my *sarathi* was a God. I knew He was. I was one of the blessed few to witness his *Virat Roop*—the beginning and the end of all creation."This is your *dharma*," He said, smiling. I was nothing more than a tool—an instrument of righteousness, chosen to vanquish evil. "My job is to guide," He preached. "Yours is to act. Walk the path before you. Leave the rewards and punishments to me."

So I picked up my fallen bow and followed the path he laid out. I walked the road of righteousness. Family, friends, lifelong loyalties—none of them mattered to the bow in my hand, an unerring, unrelenting weapon of justice. I banished childhood memories as my chariot cut through the battlefield. Memories of playing with cousins in the open fields, sitting on my uncle's lap, eating treats from my aunts' kitchens. Warm, precious fragments of a past that had no place in a war waged for *dharma*.

I was on the side of good. But was I good? Now, as I watch His stiff back, the doubts claw their way in again. I miss the reassurance in his smile as my enemy falls.

It wasn't a fair fight. He was unarmed, off his chariot, struggling with its wheel. He never saw the arrow coming.

Did he feel death approaching? Did the wind whisper something in his ear as he took his final breath? Did the earth open her arms to welcome him?

I hope she did. He was a loyal friend, the son of the mighty Sun God, and a warrior unlike any other. Perhaps the best of us all.

By birth and strength alone, he should have been crowned emperor. But he declined—not out of ambition or lack thereof, but because his loyalty lay elsewhere.

History may call me the greatest warrior. I am not. There were others—far more gifted, far more deserving. But they were sacrificed along the way, like the warrior now lying face down in the earth.

The title is hollow. The road to it is bloody and treacherous.

I only wish my hands weren't bound by *dharma*. I wish I hadn't been the chosen one—the one blessed and burdened to witness the divine in his magnificent cosmic form.

I wish I were a nameless foot soldier. Or perhaps a poor farmer—free to love and repay kindness with kindness.

Parikshit, Build a Better Tomorrow

Parikshit, my son. Seeing you play in the place grounds is such a delight to my old weary eyes. Your smile is the only thing that replaces the sight of the mighty Pandavas with their heads hung in despair and their weapons at their feet.

My son, just as I see the future in you, you see the past through my eyes. So what should I tell you? Should I tell you about your grandfathers' failure to protect their son, or the bravery of your young father?

History is something that happened in the past and that shapes our future your gurus will teach you. They are wrong. History is what we choose to let you and the others see. We, the guardians of the past, pick and choose the lessons you can learn. We, the Pandavas did win the great battle of good over evil, but both good and bad reside in your heart. As hard as you might try, you cannot banish one from your heart without the other. Sing songs of glory for your father and your grandfathers, but do not let the world forget Dhuryodhan's kindness, Karana's loyalty and Gandhari' s sacrifice. Be humble and remember the mistakes and wrongs that your family did and when possible atone for our sins.

Embrace the lessons of our collective past, my dear Parikshit. Understand that it is both the light and the darkness that shape our legacy. Only through this awareness can you forge a future where compassion triumphs over conflict, and wisdom guides your every decision. Son, you carry the bravery of Arjuna and the divinity of Krishna in your blood. Let that be your strength. Build a kingdom where the goodness in our hearts always prevails—so that your children, and theirs, never have to witness another Kurukshetra.

Love

The sun slipped behind the mountains, and darkness began to creep in.. The conversation was punctuated with extended silences. It was time to leave. The thought of leaving gave her the courage to ask the question she'd been holding back."

"Do you love him still?"

The response was a sad smile. Maybe the question did not have an answer. She wasn't sure. It was a long time before she spoke.

"My father said the Gurus are wise and must be obeyed. His Guru said that the fates said he marry me, so we were married. The king, his father exiled him, and like a dutiful son, he took me to the forest. He played the role of a provider, a protector and a spiritual guide for the fourteen years. Most of what I know of Dharma today was learnt over dinner in our humble hut. A wife's honour demanded I wait for him, so I sat on the doorstep of a hut and waitied to be rescued. The king's honour demanded I walk through fire. I was forsaken for the kingdom. Today he is Lord Ram, while they call me Sita Ma. Even the titles people bestowed build a wall between us.

Love never played a role in our life together, duty and honour did. Here in this small hut at the edge of the forest, my love for him or the lack of it is irrelevant."

Meet Sputnik

Meet Sputnik, an incredibly joyful dog. You may wonder why anyone would think he could be unhappy. After all, he lives in a lovely home, enjoys healthy meals on time, and receives tons of attention and love.

I disagree.

Sputnik, the dog, does not see time–and its steady march–the same way as you and I. There are definitely moments when he's hungry, and it feels like no one's paying attention. But in those moments, he relies on something deeper: a quiet inner strength. He trusts that food will eventually arrive. He has this rock-solid faith in his family's love, even if they don't play with him as much as he'd like or sleep in, delaying his morning walks.

He's also pretty good at letting things slide–like when someone accidentally steps on his tail or gives him a bath. Everyone knows how much he hates getting soaked with water and soap. Yet they still carry him, smiling, into the bathroom. His cries, and the fact that he hides under the bed, have no impact.

These are things he does not like. But the thing he really hates... is a suitcase.

When he sees one, it always means someone is about to leave. That makes him anxious—because he doesn't know who it'll be or when they'll return. Still, he stays loyal, waiting patiently with his ear pressed to the door.

No, Sputnik does not *know* all will be well.

But he trusts that his world will still be there in all the tomorrows to come. And in that, he finds his happiness.

Let us all be a bit like Sputnik.

Party, Food, Fun and Prison

Look, look at all these humans–sitting around, enjoying themselves; eating, drinking, sniffing each other's butts, shaking hands, and ignoring me.

Lively music plays, and I'm sure they hear me–they just don't listen to my cries. They keep talking and laughing while I sit here, locked in my tiny crate! I can hardly breathe, and the floor hurts my delicate bum. The human bought a memory foam mattress. I wonder why–and what a mattress needs to remember. Anyway whatever makes the humans happy.

What did I do to deserve this? I just got a tad excited over a guest and sprayed a little pee on the carpet. Isn't that what carpets are for? To soak up pee and the drinks I spill? And before you ask–I did knock over a glass or two, and yes, I ate a few appetizers from someone's plate. They were a little smelly, but I'm not picky. "Not good for your tummy," they say. Then why have them in my house, I ask you!

And what is the deal with hiding the shoes? They make amazing snacks. One of the guests looked upset because I chewed a bit of her fancy shoe. Well, maybe she should've known: shoes are treats, not accessories to be carried on your feet.

Do I hear someone calling for me? Yeah, that's for me, alright. Gotta run—I need to take the big human for a walk now.

A dog's work is never done.

Loving and Loved

Sputnik is a loved member of the family. The youngest, the cutest and the most huggable, this is no surprise. His needs are considered before planning any vacation or even a dinner out. If he decides to laze around in the house, plans are changed to accommodate him.

There is another side to this golden coin though. He took his time with potty training and still occasionally shows his disappointment by leaving a 'gift' once in a while. He ate a very expensive shoe, belonging to a guest. Reason? We left him home alone for way too long, or maybe he did not like the treat. I have a feeling that we spent too much time with the guest and he did not like that. We are his people, and in his own way he is possessive about us. Anyway, you get the picture.

Loving and living with Sputnik isn't always a walk in the park.

So why does our universe revolve around his tilted head? Simple! Lack of expectations. I do not expect him to get a certain grade in school. His wagging tail is enough to brighten my day. My son does not expect him to help with his homework or to be his wing man, nor does my husband want him to clear his coffee mug. Every small gesture is appreciated and loved. Yes, even the half-eaten shoes lying across the living room floor is a source of joy (after a lot of time and guilt pass away.

Sputnik embraces each moment with a sense of purpose rather than treating them as mere routines. Whether it's enjoying a meal, taking a stroll in the park, or even the simple act of bending down to scratch his ears, he responds with heartfelt gratitude. He senses our affection in countless small interactions throughout the day and strives to ensure we feel that same love in return. In a world filled with expectations and pressures, Sputnik reminds us that sometimes the simplest joys—like a wagging tail or a playful nudge are most profound, teaching us to cherish the present and relish the bond we share.

And this, my dear, is how we should define love!

Why I love Poop !!

It was early morning. I say "early morning" because I was up before the sun. Let's all graciously overlook the fact that it's a winter morning in Europe, where the sun takes its sweet time to embark on its daily stroll across the sky. Regardless, in my book, being out of bed before sunrise and before the coffee kicks in is nothing short of an Olympic sport. And there I was, training for gold, still in my pyjamas, with hair that could easily pass for a startled hedgehog.

As I brushed my teeth, a horrid smell assaulted my nose–a heady cocktail of rotting food, manure, and a generous splash of ammonia. My nose wrinkled in disgust, but, oddly enough, the corners of my mouth curled upward in reluctant amusement. That's Sputnik for you–my puppy–and his signature morning gift to the household.

I couldn't help but wish I'd woken up earlier to save everyone from this olfactory assault. You see, Sputnik is still a puppy, and patience is not exactly his strong suit when it comes to waiting for his walk. As I scrubbed my teeth with the enthusiasm of a caffeine-fuelled dentist, I mulled over the possibility of toilet-training him–or better still perhaps investing in a gas mask and a lifetime supply of air freshener.

Just then, the door creaked open, and hubby dearest shuffled in, squinting like a bewildered owl. "If you don't figure out a solution soon," he declared, "we might as well start charging admission for the 'Smell of Sputnik' experience. Complimentary nose plugs included."

I laughed, despite myself.

The smell may be unpleasant, but it's not without its silver linings. It's Sputnik's way of saying, *I'm fine, last night's dinner was great,* and *Hey, I'm healthy.* It's a daily health report wrapped in an aromatic gift.

And then there's me. My day begins with cleaning up after the one who loves me unconditionally. Sputnik doesn't care about the latest book I've read, the clothes I wear, or the size of the house we live in. This simple, humble task grounds me. No matter how much money I earn or how far I climb the social ladder, my mornings start with something as basic as cleaning up after someone I love.

It takes only a couple of minutes. Hands washed, mess gone, and just like that, the smell vanishes as quickly as it spread. As I sip my coffee, savouring its rich aroma, I reflect on the lesson Sputnik has taught me.

Every mess—no matter how big, ugly, or smelly—can be cleaned up. All it takes is a little will, some toilet paper, and a bit of soap.

No, I do not love dog poop. But I love everything it represents.

The Morning Routine

It's a wonderful dream. I am running wild and free, the green grass wet with morning dew under my cushiony paws and the wind blowing is my ears. I suddenly smell a rabbit and decide; today is the day I finally caught one, after all, all my ancestors were pros at it. Why should I be any different?

Suddenly, without a warning, something rudely drags me back into the bed. I am not on the field anymore just a moment away from becoming the great rabbit hunter. I am warm and cosy curled up in my bed at home. The dream was vivid and I was disappointed that I was no longer in the wild. As I slowly opened my eyes, I realised the house is silent barring gentle snores coming from both rooms. 'A chance for me to catch some more ZZZs' I tell myself as I settle back into the bed.

In a while, a bell rings and then footsteps go into the bathroom. Five minutes of silence and then the show begins. I began my morning pandiculation and prepare for the show. It plays for the audience of one, and I bring my A-game to it, every single morning. The lights come up in quick succession and then the background scores- the hiss of the steam iron, the low drum beats of the washing machine, the purr of the oven and the tap of the knife on the chopping board. I enjoy the sound of the water rushing with the hurried footsteps in random directions but always towards the same goal. There are short rushed monosyllabic conversations which I do not always follow. And then there is the walk – the one I enjoy but is never as long as I hope it to be. Quick kisses and four bangs of the door, one by one everyone steps off the stage and out of the house.

Me? I am left behind. I try every morning to delay or avoid the end, but just like the sun rises every morning, the curtain falls down in my home. The feeling of isolation and the desperation that follows is not something anyone would like. I curl up on a slipper that was just left by the door, trying to capture some leftover warmth. The enormous house, empty and silent, feels a little cosier when you have someone's memories to curl up to.

Beware of the Dog

"And just like that, we transformed our backyard into Fort Knox—complete with a 'Beware of Dog' sign. Of course, the only thing Princess guards is the couch cushions and her secret stash of treats. If anyone dared to approach, they'd be greeted with a ferocious bark—one that sounds more like a snack order than an actual threat."

"Hmm. Wait. What exactly are you implying? We have a dog. I have a dog. I do not lie. You know that, and frankly, I resent your insinuation."

"Do you honestly think Princess is a dog anyone needs to 'beware' of? Just the other day, she ran back inside from the balcony just because two pigeons looked at her funny. Be honest, does she look like a dog to you? Or maybe a mouse cosplaying as a dog?"

"Those pigeons were not normal! Okay? They were enormous, with crazy eyes. Murderous! And for your information, Princess can be scary. You just discriminate against her because she's small."

"Right, scary. The same way cotton balls are terrifying."

"No, no, don't give me that look. What about last month- Princess scared off that big monkey!" "And immediately dove into your lap when the monkey noticed her! Let's not forget, Princess was *inside* the entire time she was supposedly 'scaring' that monkey. But sure, let's give her credit–her tail was wagging like she'd masterminded the whole encounter. Maybe it was her sheer audacity that made her seem dangerous. Or maybe the monkey just didn't care."

"Mock all you want, but Princess has her moments. She's brave when it counts."

"Brave? Darling, Princess is brave when it comes to empty snack packets. Anything bigger than her shadow? Not so much."

"Crazy-eyed pigeons!"

"Right, let's not forget *those* villains. You know what? Maybe we should rename her–Xena, the Warrior Princess."

"You're impossible. Should I just take down the sign, then?"

"Leave it or keep it, your call. The sign doesn't matter to me. But you have to admit–"

"Save it, Mr. Honesty. I'll change the sign."

Denied

I read the single word again and again, hoping that rereading it might somehow change its meaning—or at least help me understand why, and how, the lives of two hundred and fifty men and women were deemed less valuable than mining diamonds in a hostile land.

The medical team had stopped giving me updates on the crew in the sick room. It was a kindness I appreciated. There was nothing our advanced technology and life-saving medicines could do for them now. They lay there, withering in pain, unable to sleep, watching death draw closer with each shallow, agonizing breath. The irony—our near-immortal technologies brought to their knees by a microbe older than our civilization.

The locals believe we brought the disease and death to their doorstep. I don't blame them. They had lived with the microbe for centuries—safe, healthy, thriving. Then the strangers came, and people started dropping like flies. First it was us, the miners, and then it was them. I still remember standing beside the village chief at the first funeral. A young boy, barely seven. He loved our machines, spent hours watching the engineers work.

With each death, their warmth faded. Trade routes dried up, their eyes grew hard, and their doors closed.

Finally, they denied us entry into their towns. Today, the message was clear: we had two hours to leave.

Only—we couldn't. Even if we disobeyed headquarters, we'd be stranded without food, medicine, or fuel in a matter of hours. Staying and fighting wasn't an option either. We're explorers and traders—not soldiers—and even at full strength, we'd be no match for the natives' primitive but deadly weapons and organized militias. The last update from the medical team stated that more than half my fleet was either dead or on their deathbeds. It was five hours ago.

There's a commotion outside. I hear the rat-a-tat of gunfire growing louder. Then—a deafening explosion. I toss the message from the chiefs aside and run toward the gates. What could I do when I got there? I didn't know. Still don't.

But a thought enters my mind. Maybe this is a blessing in disguise. It's better to meet my end on my feet—fighting—than to lie wasted in a bed, counting down my final breaths.

At least I fought.

Even if it was for a flawed cause.

A Little Longer than Polite

"Red makes you look happy."
"Your baby has a pizza!"
"Your dog looks thrilled to be with you."
"That salad looks healthy and tasty."
"I don't usually like tattoos, but yours is beautiful."
"Eighty and still in love."
"That was unexpected–and kind."

These are my answers to: What do I see in people?

It was almost afternoon, and the day was not going well. The evening promised worse–rescheduled meetings, missed deadlines, a thankless job full of ungrateful people. I needed a break. I needed kindness. Predictably, I started listing my good traits to my most attentive audience: the mirror.

And then a voice–my own, really–whispered back: You know what people don't see in you. But what do you see in people?

"Be the change you want to see." Much easier said than done. But that day, I took a step–a small one, but in the right direction.

So if you catch me staring across the street a little longer than politeness allows, don't worry. I'm just silently admiring something about you. Because all of us–

regardless of age, gender, clothes, job, or background—have something beautiful worth noticing.

Yes, even the teen in the corner café, sipping coffee with a cigarette. I see it. I hope one day, he does too.

Meet Me

I am neither beautiful nor ugly—well, hopefully not. I am quite short and exceedingly overweight; to be honest, I am obese. If we were to meet someday, I can assure you that you would take an extra moment to look back, maybe even twice. You simply can't help it; I am that BIG. It takes some time—quite a while—for you to truly see me: my sense of humor, my kindness, and my goodness. Gradually, over several conversations, I will start to change in your eyes—I may even come to seem cute!

My close friends and beloved sister would advise you not to judge a book by its cover. I'm okay with you judging me, whether based on my appearance or what lies within. After a few years, I've developed thick skin; stares, rude comments, and pitying looks are nothing more than water off a duck's back to me.

The challenge lies with me: I often judge my book by the cover. The result is not pretty—I see flaws, some real and some imagined, and each one stares back at me, unblinking and unforgiving. I notice the rolls of fat hiding beneath my oversized T-shirt; I feel the pain in my knees; I see my unattractive thighs peeking out from a lovely dress, and I hear the anguish in my light-hearted banter. I see everything, and I would prefer to hide.

Today, I finally decided to stand in front of the mirror and confront my flaws one by one. Beneath the tears and pain, I finally discovered myself—the self I often ignored or had forgotten existed, waiting for me to recognise her. Isn't it strange? I have spent my life crying for others to see the real me, yet I never took the time to see her myself. That is life: we spend a lifetime searching for something that already resides within us.

I am neither beautiful nor ugly. In fact, I might just be one of the most beautiful people you will meet today!

Today, This Moment

As I sit here my pen pauses on the paper, ready to write yet unmoving. It is not as if I do not know what to write – I have thoughts to share, wisdom to impart and tales to narrate, but I can't settle on one. Is today the day for a tender romance, or a letter to a younger self? Maybe I can share some of my experiences or tears even. Do I talk about the goodbyes I regret or the new beginning on the horizon? Perhaps, like my life, I let the words flow, without a planned route and the always painful but important grammar check. Let us see what adventures lay ahead in the next few lines. A tender kiss, a scary cry, tears, smile, introspection or merely a few moments spent well!

There are two kinds of people and we have all met the first kind, maybe few of you are those blessed people even – people who know what they are and where they need to be. Their life's are perfectly mapped and they march ahead purposefull and fearless.

The second kind is me – we flow with life, make lemonades when we have lemons, play in the sun and shiver in the cold, but forever in motion, settled but not really there. We never have both feet strong on the ground – one either lingers on days past or, already in motion for the next adventure. We may be travellers or couch potatoes – the next adventure can be an archaeological dig to find Atlantis or a new recipe of chocolate muffins. Life for us is a stream and we sit on a raft moving along sometimes rapidly and other times placidly. We meet people, do things and move on. Do not mistake this for lack of attachment. At every curve we hope for calmer waters and a chance to put in roots, but life often throws a curve ball. We miss people, cry over lost opportunities and pray for life to drop its relentless pace for a little while. We look back over our shoulders more than we care to admit. Life for us is not easy, we are not blessed with the certainty of our path. Each crossroad is a decision for us too. So, what keeps us moving? What keeps us from deciding what we are and then working towards it?

It is a steadfast belief – we are what we are supposed to be in this moment.

Today I am a mother and wife, nothing more, nothing less. Yesterday no matter how loved and tomorrow no matter how exhilarating, do not matter.

Tell the World My Tale

'Tell my tale', 'Let the world know my story' you cry in my head. 'Tell the world who I am' you say, over and over again like a broken record. The cry haunts me in my dreams and lingers with me every moment I am awake.

I hold the wooden panther in my hands. It is beautiful and my fingers glide on the smooth curves, the bright specks of colour are a feast for my weary eyes. "Who are you?" I give in. Are you a toy a young girl cherishes, or a prized possession on a rich man's mantlepiece ? Does your tale involve a poor man working under a lamp all through the night? Or, maybe you are a prince trapped in the wooden panther by an evil witch? Are you good, bad, evil or a mute spectator like me? Do you save someone or do you patiently wait for your saviour? Does this posture you are frozen in begin or end your adventure? What makes you special, your angry and powerful stance, or the smooth polished wood that shapes your body? I would say it is the details that the artist carved into you. But then, I could be wrong.

The possibilities are endless and your stories limitless. So, where shall I begin? Maybe I will grab a blank paper and a pen and let you narrate the tale!

Why I Miss Work

After nearly a decade of freelancing and working sporadically from home, I still long for the experience of going to an office. While the regular paycheck and office colleagues are certainly part of the reason, the story is much more than that.

I don't miss the frantic early morning rush–who would? The sound of the alarm and the hurried scramble to get to the office on time! However, I did appreciate the regular schedule that work provided. Since my colleagues almost always up being my friends, working from home significantly limited my friend circle. They were people like me, who got me and more often than not loved to bitch about the same person - the BOSS!

The thing I miss the most, however, is beyond the financial freedom and comradeship. It is me. At work, I am something beyond a wife and a mother. The good, the bad and the ugly; it is all me. I am judged on my performance and a smile would not always fix my troubles unlike at home. I do have a smile that can melt the frostiest heart. Life at home is happy and comfortable but here I am always in a supporting role. The mother raising her kid to be ready for life. The dutiful wife, walking alongside the husband, supporting his dreams. The daughter or the daughter-in-law fulfilling her role in the world.

At work I can be the hero in my story. The work pressure, office politics, and the stress may not be welcome, but they are mine, not inherited from the husband, the son or the family. The colours I paint are as bright or as dull as I desire. I may not always love the end product, but I sleep well with the knowledge that it was a job well done. The tears of my failure sometimes taste sweeter than the celebrations of my family's successes.

Don't get me wrong, I love my family but, sometimes I yearn for a little slice of me too!